Gemini Tales

Dedication

To the one that almost got away............

I loved you ever since I first laid my eyes on you praying for the day of us to be together. From your smile, to your encouraging words you have stolen my heart. I've seen your drive and how you don't let anything stand in your way. Always speaking positivity into existence, pushing me, motivating me to follow my dreams and giving me the love that I had been missing out on. Thank you for believing in me and entrusting me with your heart. Locked in with you for life..............

Love you always,

Your Baby

<u>Dontae</u>

It's Friday the 13th and my movie came out today "Never Sleep Alone II" hmmm, I should leave work early. Being the 'Head Banker In Charge' I should've worked from home today, damn decisions, decisions, stay and risk someone agitating me or leave early and pamper myself, hmmm?

"Ehhh hmm, Ms. Richardson there's a gentlemen here requesting to speak with a supervisor." (Oh well guess I got my answer)

"Ok send him in Ava, Thank you."
"Here you are sir Ms. Richardson will take care of you."

As i'm sitting in front of my computer waiting to see what sob story someone is about give me this time, I hear the voice "Thank you for seeing me Ms. Richardson" I lift my eyes up from my computer and here we have a 6ft Caramel Chocolate athletic build, apple cap wearing, clean cut, no piercing, prettiest whitest teeth I've ever seen for a man standing in my doorway. I stand up and shake his hand.

"Hello my name is Dontae Jefferson and there's a major issue with my account."

"Ok, have a seat Mr. Jefferson and explain to me what's going on with your account."

"Please call me Dontae. I deposited two checks on Monday and they're still not showing in my account."

"Rest assured Mr. Je... I mean Dontae I will get to the bottom of this for you."

45mins later*

"Ok Dontae, problem is solved and here is your current balance. The issue was human error. The underwriting department put your checks into the banks personal account rather than yours, but I have taken care of everything and any fees that you may have incurred have been reversed. Once again I do apologize for any inconvenience this has caused you."
"Thank you so much Ms. Richardson."

"Please call me Gina."

"Well Gina, may I have your number to call you sometime?"

"Although you are flattering, i'm sorry but I don't mix business with pleasure, I hope you have a wonderful day."

He nods his head and walks off. Whew that man was sexy, "Hey Ava, i'm going to lunch be back in a hour."
****

Glad Jay had a opening cause I sure was lacking on my waxing. Ya girl was looking like a chia pet down there, but now she bald and smooth as a baby ass! I walk back into my office and there's this beautiful vase filled with a dozen multicolored roses with a card that read: "Thank You for all your help,

I saw these and thought of you..
Sincerly Tae." Wow this man is
really trying. As i'm reading the
card again and smelling these
beautiful long stem roses there's a
knock on my door. "Come in, Well
hello again." I turn around and
standing there is Dontae holding a
"Thank You" care bear, a single
rose, and movie tickets.

"Dontae thank you for the flowers
but..."

"Gina listen, you are a beautiful
woman and I'm taking you out
tonight to show my appreciation,
now what time shall I pick you up?
Movie starts at 8:15, call me when
you're almost ready."

 He handed me the bear, rose and
tickets (which was to the movie I
wanted to see) then kisses my

hand. "My number is on the bear" and turns and walks off. When I say ya girl was standing there stuck and ready to get her freak on, one gust of wind up my skirt and i'm fuckin up the floor. I hurry up and sit my ass in my chair twisting and turning crossing my legs back and forth pussy lips rubbin together getting wet all while staring at his number..

****

6:15 "Hello Dontae, this is..."

"I know who this is, The Beautiful Gina, so what time am I picking you up?"

"7:45, I live in those apartments overlooking the beach. My address is 9450 Red Apple Dr. 12th floor, but i'll meet you in the foyer."

****

It's 7:50 let me take my ass down to this lobby. As i'm getting off the elevator Dontae is just walking in the building. He sees me and says "You have the most amazing glow Gina" he reaches for my hand and walks me to a candy coated Royal Blue 2013 Infiniti Truck sitting on 25 inch rims with mirror tint. He opens the door (yes ladies chivalry is not dead) I get in, he hops in the other side and we're off to the movies.

It was a short drive I only lived 10mins from the theatre. Once we park he hops out quickly rushes to the passenger side and opens the door for me. Such a gentleman. He grabs my hand and escorts me into the movie theatre. Now my phone been dry all week but since i'm on a date it's blowing up non stop, but I ignore it cause my focus is on Dontae. The movie was pretty good, kinda scarey which made me cuddle up on him. After the movie was over he brought me back home.

 "Tae do you mind walking me inside and looking around i'm kinda scared?"

He laughs, "So you want to sacrifice me? Ok, I got you."

We go inside luckily the elevator is already on the first floor, he follows me to my apartment, I open the door and he goes in cuts all the lights on and does a walk thru;

 "Ok all clear Gina."
"Thank you so much.. umm would you like to stay, we could talk and

have a drink if you like."

"Sure Gina"

"Please sweetheart call me Gigi"

"Alright Gigi."

I pour us two drinks and lead him to my bedroom. Tae sits in the chair as I change my clothes, getting comfortable. I mean I feel so safe with him that I let my guard down and just spilled my guts telling him absolutely everything about me keeping it 100. Tae stands up comes behind me and asks..

"Gigi what do you see in the mirror?"

"I don't know."
"Well I see a woman who has been hurt, misunderstood, that needs to be held and made love to."

Lost in his words I feel his lips on the side of my cheek then he turns me around and kisses me. Caught me completely off guard taking my breathe away. Dontae pulls me closer and I could feel his hard dick pressed up against me. All I could think was i'm glad I got my pussy waxed today. I pulled away from him and his dick is bulging out. Dontae grabs my hand and glides it to his manhood. Then moves my hand to his belt which I unbuckle, unfasten his pants and they just fall straight to the floor. He pulls his dick out which I must say was perfect. I go in my night stand and pullout a flavored condom which he puts on. He kisses me, i'm pushing him down on the bed and start sucking his dick. I hear little subtle grunts here and there coming from Dontae.

"Oh Shit that feels good baby but the rubber too tight."

I let his dick fall out my mouth, take the condom off, and now he is 10 times bigger. I start slobbing on his manhood again, hearing him moaning and laying back on the bed while rubbing my head, I know this nigga ready to bust. I stand up, he grabs my arm and lays me down on the bed "My turn to taste you!" Kissing my body from head to toe, moving back up to my pussy, maneuvering his tongue very slow teasing me while slowly inserting it in my vagina. This man has me quivering cause gettin your snatch ate after a fresh wax is unexplainable. (If you haven't gotten one GO GET ONE, you missing out boo, thank me later!) I feel like I have to pee so I push his head away but now the feeling leaves. He gets up and I scoot back in the bed, now climbing on top and trying to insert his dick inside me but i'm just that tight he thinks i'm a virgin. So he takes his time working that dick in slow strokes, which is making me wetter and wetter. "TTTaaeeee i'm about to cum". Going deeper and stroking faster, pushing my leg back into the bed, my hot juices spewing out.

 Oh shit I gotta pee!

 I'm trying to utter the words out but it feel so damn good I don't want him to stop while not tryin to pee the bed. My other leg now pushed back and the next stroke hits my sweet spot. Instant pissin in the bed and it won't stop but feels so damn good. I've never pee'd before where it drove me crazy to the point i'm clawing up a nigga back and screaming at the top of my lungs.

"Gigi you ready for me to cum baby?"

"YES Tae cum for me please."
Tae spreads my legs all the way to the side as if I were doing a split and pounds my pussy hard makin me piss once again, his cock gettin harder and bigger stretching my kat like she has never been stretched before. He's shaking, sweat dripping down his nose, roles over and kisses me on my forehead. Feeling wonderful but mad at the same time cause this nigga done made me urinate in my bed.
"Tae GET UP! I gotta change my sheets and clean my mattress you

made me piss the fuckin bed!"

He chuckles.

"What's so damn funny? This not a laughing matter."
"Are you serious Gigi?"
"Do it look like i'm joking?"

"Gigi for real you can't be serious. SO you've never squirted before?"

"Yea I did it in your face."

"No baby, that wasn't squirt you got extra wet. When you thought you were pissing you were actually squirting. That's why it felt so good and also explains why that shit was dripping off the bed because it was your first time."

In disbelief I smell the bed and nope no piss just sweet and sticky.

"Yes baby I popped yo cherry and made you cream."

"Whatever Tae no you didn't."

He pushes me back down on the bed and starts eating my pussy again and I instantly turn into a water hose, gets up flips me over rams his dick in my pussy now I turned into a damn super soaker 5000. It's so much that his dick slips out, Tae puts it back in but it slid in my ass instead. Oh shit that's the wrong hole but it feels so good. He starts to stroke but I can't take it and he pulls out, my squirt falling like a faucet is on. I'm stuck in doggystyle he pulls my legs so I can fall on the bed.

"Tae what the fuck just happened?"

"I made you squirt for the very first time and took your ass virginity, lol.

I POPPED YOUR CHERRY! You are welcome GOODNIGHT!"

Keisha

With the sun beaming on my face who needs a alarm clock. Laying in this bed alone feels so good & bad. Wouldn't mind rolling over into some big strong arms with a nice rock hard 12inch dick winking at me. Now i'm rubbing on my clit getting super wet caressing my breast. I hit my spot and all my warm juices come spilling out. Thinking damn that was good! Next thing I know my phone ringing. Oh is it my dream about to come true? Answering the phone in my sexy voice

"Hello"

"Girl wake up, you know what time it is? What day it is?"

"Hey Candance." Now Candance

(Candy as we call her)is my sister, and today is her bachelorette party. "Yes Candy, I know today Cinco de Mayo," laughing...
"Bitch stop playing with me!"

"Okay Okay I know"

"What time you gonna be at Keisha house?"

"Well since I have to help her set up I'll be there at 5pm. Okay, bye, see you later." Shit couldn't even enjoy my damn orgasm. Oh well let me get up and get started.

I'm headed to Keisha house. Keisha is Candy best friend since they were 10. So it's only right she's her maid of honor and hosting the party, plus Keisha has this big ass 4bedroom house with a whole boom boom room with a full bar in her basement. I pull up and

Keisha outside doing the absolute most with the decorations. I tried to help but she finished already. "Gigi can you help me with setting up downstairs? Yea I got you." So I follow her to the boom boom room. She remodeled since I was last there. This chic got a stripper pole in there with a little stage with mirrors behind it. I'm standing there with my mouth open in a trance and she snap her finger..

"EARTH TO GIGI you good?"

"Yea girl when you do this?"

"Last month you know I like to get it poppin. Come on we got about 2 hours before people start showing up."

"Okay what you want me to do?"

"Just help me set the food up." As we doing this her ass flips the punch bowl all over herself and gotta change.

I'm cleaning the mess up while she shower. Yelling from upstairs. "Hey Gigi which outfit should I wear?" I go in her room and she got three outfits laid out. She starts trying them on. Each outfit shows off her every curve. Keisha was a bad bitch! 5ft, long black hair, 40DDD, 30 hips, 38 waist. Thick thick. My nipples started poking out looking at her and i'm twisting and turning on her bed. Keisha notices and asks me "what's wrong, am I making you uncomfortable?" I'm thinking no it's the total opposite, I'm wet as fuck! Keisha walked up on me and just start rubbing my titties. Should I stop her, ask her what she doing, nope I was froze. She steps back, her dress top falls, walks back to me place her perfect titties in my face and I start licking her aereola. She rubs my nipples while whispering "I want you to FUCK ME!" She pulls her dress off and climbs in the bed spreading her legs open. Her pussy was so pink and pretty glistening from all her wetness. I start kissing on her thighs while she squirming. Kissing the top of her pussy and go to the other thigh. This is teasing her making her drip now. "Gigi please I can't take it anymore." But I like to play, so going from her thighs to her titties, sucking on her nipples, while rubbing her clit in between my fingers. She's getting wetter and wetter begging me to make her cum. I teased her enough so I let my tongue go down between her titties over her navel straight to her clit. It's fat too, poking out. I'm licking, suckin and smackin on it, now i'm sliding my fingers in and out of her super soaked pussy. It taste so good like peaches, and I love peaches. Now I really have my face buried in her pussy. She starts grinding that phat muthafucka in my face, "Yes baby that's my spot, I'm about to cum" she geysering all in my mouth. Whole time I was grinding my pussy on the bed and i'm cumin too. I kiss her thighs again and as i'm getting up to wipe my face she kisses me push me down and we 69. I mean she riding my face and fingering my pussy then she reaches over turns on her rose puts it on my clit. I start cumin all over her sheets, that must have turned her on cause she started riding my tongue even faster and turned into Niagara Falls. It was like a bucket of water was dumped on the bed. Now she pulling out her double ended dildo and just as she was about to put it in her we hear ding dong. That damn doorbell and people started showing up. Of all days they decide NOT to be on CP TIME. "FUCK I was just getting started!" Laughing as she get out the bed.

Carl

   "Girl what is you wearing tonight? I know you gonna be naked cause you always only wear a piece of dental floss! Ha, ha, wait hold on i'm getting another call. Hello"

"Hey babe what you doing tonight?"

"Me and Nicole going out for drinks can I see you afterwards?"

"Naw babe the fellas from the job gonna be here."

"Ok Carl i'll talk to you later bye

babe."

"My bad Nikki that was Carl I thought I was gettin some tonight.

"Gina wait, how you not getting no dick and you got a ENTIRE man?"

"Yea I know, but that side dick hit different. Ok let me get off this phone so I can finish getting ready see you at 7 bye!"

"Gigi baby where you at?"

"Tae i'm in the bathroom."

"What you about to do?"

"Told you I was going out with Nikki. We going to our reggae spot."

"AGAIN? This the 4th weekend in a row, are yall fuckin? cause cut a nigga in lbvs."

"Naw baby we just having girl time.

Besides when you working nights, I be lonely, so I go drink with her, come home, pass out and next thing I know you home sliding in this wet pussy. I thought you like how I be after hanging with Nikki."

"You right Gigi, ok baby i'm bout to get outta here for work."

"Ok love you see you in the morning."

"Love you too Gigi let me know you made it in safe."

"Ok bye before you late"

Shit I thought his ass would never leave. Let me finish getting ready. I gotta meet her in a hour, now what should I wear? Gotta be something sexy just incase I see bae tonight. Lets see, yes lowcut Seahawks jersey dress, open toe stilettos and my light green bra that snaps in the front with matching boy shorts. Yea bae love the way this bra hold my titties up. I mean shit they are a 44G, how could you not love them, especially with this bra giving them the perfect boost. Now a little eyeshadow, that natural beauty killem everytime. Standing in the mirror 'Ok bitch you looking like a whole meal!'

****

"Hey Nikki you here yet?"

"Yea i'm sitting at the bar"

"Ok cool i'm walking in"

"Hey girl your drink already ordered I got us the big one. So Gigi whats up with Carl?"

"He playing games, give me good

dick then disappear, thought I had his ass on lock but guess not."

"Well Gigi what are you doing wrong?"

Bartender: "Can I get you ladies something to eat?"

"Not right now. Well Gigi sound like you don't know what to do with that!"

"I'm trying lets get another drink."

(my phone rings) "Hello, hey baby my bad I forgot to text you when I made it, yea ok I promise to call when I get home bye! Girl Tae know he can fuck a wet dream."

(ding ding ding) "Damn Gigi who is that now?"

"Oh thats Carl lets take a pic. Dang you all up in my face an shit look like we kissing."

"Good don't you want some dick?
He gonna be all for it so take the
fuckin picture!"

"Ok it's sent"

 5mins later, "Hey baby where you
at who that with you?"

"It's my girl Nikki we around the
corner from your house."

"Okay you comin thru?"

"I can"

"Let me get the guys out and you
can come over"

The biggest smile comes across my
face and I tell Nikki we gotta finish
these drinks, pay the tab and leave.
I gotta be followed around the
corner to Carl house cause i'm lil.
Nikki gets in her car and follows
me 2mins to his house, seriously we
could've actually just walked. But

we park and she follow me to his building.. Carl is downstairs waiting and lets us in. This 6'3 peanut butter skin tone, brown eyes, muscular tone, white shorts, no boxers man leads the way to his 3rd floor apartment. Go in and we all sit down. Before Carl could get a word out I pounce on him like a cheetah. I mean I climb on top of him and start tonguing him down, kissing on his ears while grinding my pussy on his dick. The whole time Nikki just watching and I lowkey like to be watched so I know I gotta put on a show. Grinding on him got me so wet, I start to moan, he grabs my hair pulls my head back and kiss me on neck while caressing my titties. I cum instantly all over his shorts. I get up and pull his dick out his shorts and kiss it, lick the shaft up and down while twirling my tongue. Tickling his balls in my mouth. He grabs my head looks me in my eyes and say "Stop playing and suck this dick!" I look over at Nikki and she laughing "Bitch you heard him!" I opened my mouth and begin to suck that dick. I'm taking Carl all in my mouth but I couldn't get the full 10inches down my throat. Nikki see me struggling and comes over to me and says to gag. When I gag my throat will open up and then he will slide down my throat with no problem. I followed her advice and sure enough I had his dick so far down my throat he was touching my tonsils. I was hitting all them spots, Nikki stepped back and watched her girl go to work. I'm slurping on that dick so loud being nasty with it. Slob coming down on all sides his balls catching all of it, caressing his balls while suckin his dick. "Oh Fuck Gigi you being a nasty lil hoe you know I love that shit". There's another moan but it's from Nikki. She's on the couch playing with her pussy making herself cum. That made Carl dick even harder. He pushed my head down so far that I swear his dick was in my stomach, but I'm a muthafuckin troopa so I kept swallowing that dick. I guess me not snatching my head back caught him off guard cause he let out a little shriek like a bitch and said "Gigi I'm bout to bust" I give two more slow long sucks and flick my tongue he snatches his dick out my mouth and cums all over my face. That shit turned Nikki on so much she squirts, and walks over to me, kisses me just so she can taste Carl cum. She then tells me she'll holla at me later and disappears into the hallway with the door closing quietly behind her. Carl looks me in the eyes and say "YOU a bad bitch go head lay down and sleep some of that liquor off." He got dressed and left me in his house to catch up with the guys. Me being satisfied from making him cum all over my face I followed his orders and went to sleep.

Sondra

I ain't doing nothing today.
Laying on this couch and watching
tv will be my day!' Soon as I say
this shit my phone buzzes.

"Hello!"

"Whats up Gigi, what you doing?"

"Hey Eric, whats up? It's a lazy day
for me."

"Well i'm at work and my girl here
from out of town. Can you pick her
up and she hang with you?"

"Ughhh aight."

Now I gotta get in the shower and
put on some clothes, smdh! Quick
shower and slide on a pair of
leggings, bra, and jacket, screw a
shirt i'm coming right back

anyway.

 I'm taking this long ass drive to 3rd & Clifton to pick her up. I need some riding music and a redbull then I should be good for the ride. I pull up 30mins later, after fighting all the sunday drivers that like doing 45mph in the far left passing lane which is 60mph. Anyway, I get to the parking lot and there she is standing there looking like a lost puppy dog. She's not bad looking bout 5ft, 38DD, 32waist, 38hips, light skin and even though the red hair didn't fit her, she was still cute. She gets in, hugs me and thank me for getting her out the house. I'm thinking to myself as if I had a choice. Got back to my apartment and tell her to get comfortable. I start folding clothes, listening to pandora.

"Gigi, I'm sorry but you have some huge titties. Can I please touch them?"

Now how could I turn down such a face. I unsnapped my bra from the front and she cupped my right titty in both her hands, cause yes, you have to use two hands for these girls! Anyway, she starts flickin her tongue across my nipples, making them stick straight out. That shit got me dripping wet to the point you can see the wet spot in my pants. She slide her hand down my leggings and eased her finger in my pussy, and with 3 quick thrust, I'm cummin all over her fingers. I lay back on the bed and she pulls my clothes off, spreads my legs open and starts licking my clit ever so slow. Sondra letting that tongue lap up and down on my pussy, fuckin it with her tongue and kissing my clit at the same time. OMG, this shit driving me crazy! I grab the back of her head and push her face in my twat even more. She licked and twirled her tongue and I came all over her face and it's not stopping! She steady licking my clit while fingering me til I shake uncontrollably. I'm like 'Oh, its like that! Ok, my turn! I flip her ass over and slurp her pussy like my life depended on it. You know the old skool milkshakes, where you be slurpin for 10mins before you get the first taste thru the straw? Yea, that's how I went in on her clit! That was her spot cause she turned into a straight fountain. Then, I slide my dildo in her pussy while licking it and she is calling out my name in ecstasy. I roll over holding the dildo in her ocean pussy, making her ride it and then I start licking her clit. This is a sensation she never, ever had, because she is squirting like somebody left the faucet running. I mean baby girl ain't stopping! She utters out "hand me your phone." So I give it to her. She starts recording me eating her pussy and tells me to send it to Tae. For real? ok. I send the clip to Tae with the caption "GET HERE NOW". I get up and all her juices is dripping down my face. I go in the bathroom, wash my face, brush my teeth and then start cooking. Meanwhile, she in the bathroom freshening up and rolling up a blunt.

While the food simmering, I go back in the bathroom with her and we start smokin. In comes Tae and his eyes just buck out his head with the biggest koolaid smile ever. He looks at Sondra standing there butt naked and ask her if he could kiss her.

"Why would you want to do that?"

"Because I want to thank you for getting her shockras back in order."

She smiles, sticks her tongue out and he leans in and tongues her down. Now, I'm smoking watching this and she unfastens my robe and start rubbing my nipples. They start perking up she stop kissing Tae and starts to kiss me with her fingers sliding in and out of me. Sondra stops all of a sudden and saids "This not right i'm with Eric." Of course I had to say something ignorant to break this unwanted tension.

"Sondra you know the saying What happens in Vegas stays in Vegas?

"Yea"

"Well consider this Vegas!"

She looks at me then over at Tae bats her eyes, smile and blurts out "Well I guess i'm in vegas" and sashays out the bathroom and go jump in the bed with her legs eagle spread. Since I already had my turn I let Tae have some fun first. Now while he's busy with his face inbetween her legs I climb on the bed and sit on her face. I start riding her tongue and when this dude sees how everytime he hit her spot she hit my spot in turn made his dick rock hard. Me and her cum together. He like yall ain't done. He gets up and slowly stuffs his 12inch rock hard dick in her pussy. I'm still sitting on her face and the way her tongue went in my pussy after his dick was in her I like to pass out. He start thrusting but she wasn't ready for that, I had to get up because I damn near drowned the bitch! She couldn't take it, had him flip her over and started fuckin her doggystyle. This bitch screaming so loud he pushed her head into the mattress, she biting the covers, soon as she starts quivering and her knees buckle he pulls out. Now it's my turn! He bends me over kisses my pussy slow and then give me a inch of dick at a time. That shit drives me crazy and I got soakin wet. He now strokin, strokin when suddenly he stops.

"Nigga whats wrong with you I

was about to cum!"

"SHUT UP! You get over here lay on your back, Gigi sit on her face."

I do as i'm told and she starts lickin my clit and all of a sudden Tae eases his dick all the way in me. "Oh My Fuckin God" is what flew out my mouth. I start shaking he smackin my ass while going deeper in my pussy and Sondra moving that tongue faster and faster on my clit. These two muthafuckas bout to make me have a damn heart attack. Now I feel my asshole getting wet. Wait.. this nigga pouring anal lube on me. His finger slides in my ass and I just start whimpering. It's driving me crazy and i'm begging for more.

"Are you sure?" moaning loudly "YES."

Tae reaches over and grabs the anal beads. He goes 1, 2, 3, yea baby take that 7, 8 and I started moaning calling out his name.

"Yeah baby you like that?"

"Yes daddy"" he smacks my ass again.

"Then give it to me if it feel that good give me what want! Sondra you better suck that clit like it's your last meal!"

Why the fuck did he say that? She wraps her arms around me and pulls me down on her face to the point i'm smothering her, he starts going deep and hard in my pussy while these beads in my ass just smacking it. I'm trying my best to finger her and lick her clit which makes her start cummin, then she swirl her tongue on my clit and they hit my spot at the same time, next thing he got exactly what he wanted. I started squirting to the point that shit was splashing up, down, left, right I'm cummin so hard I think I started having a asthma attack. It's so much cum she start choking but I can't move, still fuckin me he lifts me up off her face so she can breathe and with the last thrust he cums and shoves his dick so far in, that I swear it was in my stomach. He pulls out and it's just buckets and buckets of cum sliding out my pussy. I'm shaking and collapse on the bed shivering. Sondra hugs me to try to get me to stop but her titties touching me just makes me keep cumin. Tae throws a blanket over me until I calm down. He leans over kisses me and say

"Now that's One Helluva Threesome thank you baby! Ok time for her to go!

"Yes daddy be right back", as we pulling our shirts over our head.

"Just go and get back."

"Bitch lets go!" i'm saying as I push her ass out the door cause you don't keep daddy waiting.

Carlton/Carl

I know this shit is so wrong
but I just can't help myself.
Engaged to Dontae for 3 years and
been messing with Carl 1.5 years.
No i'm not gonna feel bad cause his
ass cheated on me first. What's
good for the goose is good for the
gander is the saying. And the fact
that my girls, my day ones told
this nigga that my get back ain't
shit nice so don't fuckin play with
me never registered in his thick
skull. Welp he should've listened.
That's all I could think about while
packing my bag for the weekend.
Can't believe i'm finally about to
spend a weekend with Carl. Get to

go to sleep and wake up with him.
Tae yelling from the livingroom
"Gigi you going to be late for work,
you can pack when you get home."

"I had no intentions on coming
home after work, I'm hitting the
road directly after I clock out cause
Des Moines, Iowa is a 6 hour drive.
I want to get there before it gets
dark, leaving work early at 1:30.
But i'll stop in to see you."

"Aight Gigi but this some
BULLSHIT! I don't understand why
Keisha can't just come see you. I
know, I know, she just started a
new job conveniently."

I kiss Tae as I walk out the door,
"Love you." Soon as I get in my car
Carl text me making sure i'm still
coming. I replied telling him that I
was hitting the road at 1:45. I'm

seeing the 3dots move waiting on his reply, then it finally comes thru..

"I'm staying at Dandelion Suites just give the front desk your name and they will give you the key to the room text me when you on the way."

****

Ok work day is over, said my goodbyes to Tae, just got my gas and now on the road to see Carl cause it's been 4 months since his job relocated him. Ok let me back up and explain........ I use Keisha as a scape goat to be with Carl. See Carl and Tae worked together at some point welllll actually Carl was Tae boss. And when Tae cheated I had to get him back. He needed to feel

the pain and hurt that I felt, cause
we know a man can't take the
same shit they dish out! So for me
the ultimate payback isn't smashing
one of his homies but smashing his
boss the one that sign his
paychecks, yea i'm petty and like
to play with fire, but only when
you cross me! So the way I met
Carlton is Tae bought him to our
customer appreciation carnival.
Carl is 6'3 and Tae is 6' and baby I
love a tall man something I can
climb, that gets me wet
instantaneously. They kept me
company at my little booth for the
day. Tae went to the bathroom
and Carl asked could I call his
phone cause he couldn't find it. So
he used my phone to call his, and
no I didn't think anything of it. Tae
gets back and Carl decides to leave.

I pack up my booth and leave with Tae. Later that night Carl texts me and asks if we could meet up and talk. I told him sure we can meet tomorrow at the reggae spot 5pm.

****

Next day 3:45pm 1 unread message

"Hey Gi come to my crib instead here's the address..11783 Brownlog lane
I replied, "OK"

Now tell me why this nigga stay right around the corner from the reggae spot? Coincidence, naw it was meant to be. I arrive at Carl apartment, he buzzes me up. Now this dude is on the 3rd floor and it's 97 degrees outside with a heat index of 107. Sister girl is sweating ok, glad I went commando and a front closing bra. He pours us a drink and lights a blunt. We smoke and drink i'm not a big smoker so it don't take much to get me lit. Next thing I know i'm horny and this man don't have on a shirt. He see me staring at him so he scoots closer and massages my back. Now his hands going to my breast and kissing my ears. My hands reaching for that bulge and damnit I got it. I jumped up looked at him and let my dress drop to the floor. I pull his dick out his pants and begin to suck. He's licking his lips trying to keep his composure but with my mouth being so warm he can't contain it. Grabbing the back of my head pushing it down on his dick even further, i'm slurping on it, he's trying to put his entire dick in my mouth, i'm thinking aight nigga this what you want and I gag on him spittin on his dick and jaggin it. He helps me off my knees and lead me to the bedroom pulls out a condom from the dresser puts it on. I lay down in the bed, spread my legs and he gives my pussy 3 quick licks gets up and slides his dick in me. Oh my he went straight to my spot wtf. Staring me in my eyes stroking me slow and *BEEP BEEP BEEEPPPPP* aww damn. I was day dreaming in traffic about Carl. Ok i'm 20mins away, damn I was so lost in how he came into my life that I didn't realize i'd been driving 5 1/2hrs. I pull up at the hotel and park, got the key and went in, texting Carl letting him know I was there. He was still working so I had a chance to get cleaned up. He said have something sexy on or be naked.

**2hrs later he finally comes in. I'm standing there with a black sheer top, lace thongs, stilettos, front plunge booster bra.

"Oh yea you follow instructions well I love that shit!

I pour his drink, take his clothes off and give him a long I miss you kiss. He goes and gets in the shower I follow behind him and get in. Taking the towel from him and began washing his body. Scrubbing it til the skin tried to come off cause seriously ladies who likes to smell sweaty lint covered balls i'll wait... He rinses off gets out the shower and I dry him off. Walks and lays down in the bed. I pull out my massage oil and rub him down paying special attention to his ass cause it was tense. He rolls over and I massage his thighs. I climb on top of him rubbin his head while grinding on his dick.

"G why you teasing me you know what to do with that dick."

I slide off and suck his balls, now his dick.

"Yea you like that don't you? I bet yo ass won't keep this dick away from me like this again!"

I'm licking his balls and my tongue gets close to his ass and he moans so loud. Oh you like that huh. So I go back to suckin his dick making myself gag so I can have the extra slob. I made sure my fingers were good and wet. As I went down swallowing his dick in its entirety I slid my finger in his ass.

"OH FUCK G! That feel so good baby keep going don't stop.. I'm about to nut shoot it on your face."

Yes 5 secs later I had a facial. Now he needs a few minutes to recover so I get cleaned up, go lay back on the bed, he's puttin on a condom while distracting me with the rose then stuffs his dick in my pussy stroking her while holding the rose on my clit. It was so intense I couldn't say a word, so I snatched that rose from him and threw it. I get on all fours, he comes up behind me rubbing that dick on my pussy lips, fingering me and rubbin my juices on my asshole. I feel the pressure on my ass and i'm breathing real fast and hard. In my ear I hear

 "SHHH, SHHHH, SHHHH Just breath, breath, relax, just relax" as he's whispering this in my ear, he has now inserted his dick in my ass and is slow stroking. It feels so good all of 1.5minutes but I made him stop cause it started to hurt. He stuck his tongue in my pussy and after several licks I came all over his face. It's dripping and he trying to catch it like a dog drinking out the bowl. We both lay down but I passout first.

****

7a.m. and I roll over into a puddle in the bed. I knew I was still horny last night and now I done came just that much in my sleep. His ass is knocked out and I try my hardest to wake him up but he won't budge. So I pulled out my rose and dildo. I'm hitting my spots moaning loud calling out his name and he ain't moved. Tired once again I lay on his stomach. Soon as he feels me down there he puts his dick in my mouth. I'm thinking 'Oh you want some sucky sucky? Ok nigga.' I take all of his dick in my mouth, spit bubbles blowing out the sides.

"YOU THE MUTHAFUCKIN THROAT GOAT! Yes G yo new name is 'TG' Throat Goat!"

I stop suckin his dick he hurries puttin a rubber on and I ride him reverse cowgirl. He smackin my ass while i'm ridin, toes curling. I turn back around and really bouncing on his dick slowing it down.

"Carl tell me you love me"

"I ain't saying SHIT!"

"Carlton Jacob Jones Tell me you LOVE ME!"

"Nope you gotta fuck it outta me"

"CHALLENGE ACCEPTED"

I'm rolling on his dick real slow, grinding my pussy, bouncing up and down slow while rubbing my titties. He loving this shit moaning and grabbing my hips. I slow it down even more and suck my titties..

"OH Carl IM BOUT TO CUM, CARL CARL CJ,"

"I LOVE YOU GIGI, FUCK I LOVE YOU, happy now?"
"YES"

Since I wore that ass out he gives me the black card, his car keys and tells me to take myself on a shopping spree. Hell that's music to my ears all the work I done put in I deserve to be pampered, shit! I hit up the bougie mall, yea nothing in there was under $150. Found a salon got my hair touched up, deep tissue massage and why not a pedicure. All that shopping makes you hungry and tired. I called CJ to see what he wanted to eat but he didn't answer. Well guess now he gotta spend more money and take me out, I was trynna dine in but oh well his pockets not mine lol. I get back to the hotel tried calling him again so he could help with the bags but still no answer. That's right he put his phone on silent, duh. I grab as many bags as I can and go inside. Get to the room and you could smell the weed and hear the music. I bet this nigga high as hell playing the damn game. I open the door and I hear...

"Oh daddy you like that? You like the way that dick feel in my ass?"

I closed the door behind me not making a sound putting my bags down..

"You just made that dick go all the way the fuck in!"

"Oh thank you daddy smack my ass!"

"CARL! SO this why you couldn't answer your phone you too busy gettin yo rocks off? And then you have the nerve to be fuckin a MAN LIKE FOR REAL A WHOLE MAN?" He pushes dude off him and come running grabbing my arm.

"See baby it ain't even like that i'm just confused about my sexuality."

"CJ let me the fuck go! You could've told me that's what you was into, who am I to judge. I'm just mad that you didn't tell me, you promised me you would tell me if you was fuckin somebody else, but at least you did wear a condom."

"So Gigi baby we good?"

"Yea we good Carlton."

"Why the government?"

"Cause I thought I knew you but evidently I don't therefore you are now Carlton. And don't worry I won't tell anyone, your secret is safe with me." (so yall don't tell nobody else lol)

While he was putting ol boy out I had packed my bag, grabbed all my new shit and took it to my car. Transferred the rest of the bags from his car to mine and pulled the fuck off to go home. Yes I kept the black card filled my tank up, went to the atm and took out the max. As I was on the highway driving thinking about that BULLSHIT his car keys and card went flying out the window. Easy come easy go.

"BYE CARLTON"!

Twan

It's such a nice day out. I'm glad the neighborhood got together and decided to throw a old skool block party. I wonder if everyone from back in the day is coming? Be good to see how everyone else changed. Anyway let me pull something together cause I know i'm gonna be unrecognizable. That shy girl with pigtails, braces, pigeon toe and glasses is no more. Wait til they see Gigi!

****

Ok I can get with this. 90s theme with Rodeo playing in the distance.

"Hey Gigi girl is that you? Come here! You look the same just grown. And damn you got a bangin ass body now. You had that work done?"

"Peaches hell naw girl you ain't changed. It's good to see you too." Everyone here and when I say everyone I mean EVERYONE including Twan."

Now let me explain Twan. He a couple years older than me but I had the biggest crush on him. Caramel skin, light brown eyes that change in the sunlight, just sexy as fuck with the most lickable lips ever! I never got a chance to say anything because I didn't think I was his type.

"Hey Gigi everybody over here come on"

"Iaght lets go."

EVERYBODY is here even those that dropped off the face of the earth...The exballers aka drug dealers, thugs aka fine niggas was all here representing and I can honestly say they all look the same just older some with grey but it look sexy.

"Uh oh they playing our song 'Tootsie roll' come on lets dance"

Me and Peaches getting it, we hitting every step, then next thing I know somebody rubbing all up on me getting a little too friendly. So I turn around with a attitude about to cuss whoever it is out and in my eye sight is this 5'10 muscle bound fully tatted man standing in front of me. I mean the smoothest caramel skin, beautiful full pussy eating lips. Lips so juicy look like he worships the pussy while he devours it!

"Excuse me do I know you cause you were getting a little too friendly bruh."

"Stop playing you know what it is"

"Sorry but I don't know you."

Standing here trying not to drool cause i'm staring at perfection ya here me! From fresh shoulder length locs, to the Coach glasses, muscle shirt, Coach watch, grey shorts, tone calfs... just fine, sexy, gods gift to women ok.

"Miss lady seriously you don't know who I am?"

I had to fix my eyes and step back and look, naw that can't be, hell naw it ain't. Next thing I know this man got his arms wrapped around my body and got his soft lips on mine tonguing me down. He lets me go, steps back looks me in my eyes and say

"Miss lady."

"TWAN! BABY OMG" I hug him and he starts tonguing me down again. We finally stop and was both speechless. Then I hear Peaches ass talking bout "it's about damn time! Yall both been wanting this since forever." So we start talking catching up, we exchange numbers and mingle with everyone else. Whole day i'm in a trance cause that kiss was everything.
****

What a day glad to see everyone was doing well. And Twan omg he just wow. Before I could get lost in my thoughts I get a text.....

"Hey this Twan hope you made it in safe, how about we meet tomorrow"

"Ok sounds like a plan."

I ran a hot steamy shower. Water hitting my back massaging it and I just can't stop thinking about Twan. Imagining his hands washing my body, moving slowly around my waist with his dick pressed up against me. Oh he feels so good, those fingers crawling across my thighs, now i'm super wet, fingering my soakin wet pussy, as soon as I start to cum the water gets ice cold and I snap out of it realizing he ain't here. "Damn he got me stuck" let me get out this cold shower and climb my ass in this king size bed, lay my head on the pillow closing my eyes.

 **Phone buzzin... 1 unread
message

"Good morning beautiful here's my
address..........11024 Sammie Lane,
Falcon Crest, hit me when you on
the way."

Shit I must've been extra tired
cause I didn't even remember
falling asleep. Well shit let me get
in this hot bath rejuvenate this
pussy. I'm so excited i've always
wanted Twan and it was about to
 happen, oh I hope it's all I ever
wanted. What do I wear? Highlow
fitted dress, guess tie up shoes,
front snap bra no panties.

"Hey luv eta 45minutes see you
soon"

*** 45minutes later I arrive and
park directly infront and walk up

the driveway, Twan is standing in
the door with them muscles looking
good enough to eat.. Grey jogging
pants and a wife beater showing
off them muscles and tats. This
man got me wet as fuck and I
don't have no panties on. All I can
think is please don't let me leave a
trail. I follow him to the tv room,
he pulls out a bottle of Hennessy
and say "we about to take shots
and toast to life long friends". We
 taking double shots and he got the
cranberry juice trying to pass it to
me, but see I ain't no punk so i'm
taking the shots to the head no
chasers. We finish off the bottle and
he sits back on the couch. It gets
hot because the liquor has kicked
in. He tells me get comfortable.
Pulling my dress over my head,
revealing i'm only wearing a bra,

and now my juices have started sliding down my leg. He pulls his dick out and my mouth fell open. I'm thinking where is that going. King Cobra is what he packing. 12inchs with a curve, NOT a HOOK but a muthafuckin CURVE and it's thick. Well Gigi doesn't scare easily and doesn't back down from a challenge. Kissing him allowing my tongue to slither down his rock solid chest with a little beer belly to his shaft. Letting my tongue go up, down and around his dick til I got to the tip and kissed it. My tongue swirling on the tip, his dick slide into my wet mouth, he lets out a slight sigh of pleasure.

"Oh shit Gigi its like that baby?"

"Oh you like that?"

"Yea baby I like that"

"Ok well what you think of this?"

Spitting on the head, swallowing his entire dick, curve and all. I'm sucking slow like a vacuum, slob sliding down, spit bubbles, extra sloppy toppy! No gag reflexes and when his dick touched that thang in the back of my throat he let out the most amazing moan a man could make. I got up, climbed on top of him, slowly lowering my fat dripping wet pussy onto his dick. Moving up and down so slow that each time we both let out cries of ecstasy at the same time. Riding that cobra dick, my arms behind his head pulling those dreads, kissing his ears, then those juicy as lips. I start cummin the minute he sticks his tongue in my mouth. He flipped me over and starts giving me long slow back shots. I'm cummin so damn hard my legs are tremblin. Staying on my spot making me squirt, sounding like somebody pouring water onto the carpet. Twan lays me down, kiss my inner thighs and slides that muthafuckin tongue across my clit while kissing my pussy lips. Oh baby I saw the stars, moon, sun, etc. I'm thinking this must be what heaven feels like. He annihilated my pussy, stands up with all my juices dripping from his face. Leans in so I could taste my cum on his face which is turning me on even more. I start kissing every inch of his body cause he is tatted tf up(neck, chest, arms, back, stomach, legs)! I hit that spot and he pushes my legs behind my head, sliding the cobra inside of me. I'm feeling all of his 12inches. Fucking me, rubbing my

clit, squirting everywhere
uncontrollably. My legs
being pushed into the couch turned
him on cause I felt his dick get
twice as big. We both cum
simultaneously. He gets up and I
try to stand, but my legs are like
noodles.

"Whats wrong?"

I'm still cumin" he bends me over
and starts fuckin me again.
Mounting me, Twan was able to hit
every single fuckin spot that I
started crying. It should be a crime
for dick to be that fuckin good.
Dick whip yes, most definitely. But
let me make this clear, NO
relationship this is a
DICKUATIONSHIP! Soakin wet,
creamin and cummin out my ass.
Twan collapsed on top of me
kissing me then stands up and

smacks my ass.

"Yea baby imma be needing that."

"Ok, hey Twan got a question.."

"Whats up babes?"

"As far as my head game how did I do?"

"Baby you most definitely in the top 3, Hell baby you #1! Ain't nobody ever been able to swallow that muthafuckin curve like you."

I got dressed and he gave me another long kiss before I left. "Call me when you make it home."

Keisha

I walk up behind Keisha palming both her titties, caressing each one while flicking my fingers over her nipples, giving gentle kisses on her neck. She starts moaning I lift her arm up to put around my neck. One hand still caressing her rock hard nipple while my other hand glides down the side of her body slowly sliding inbetween her thighs. Keisha is now biting her bottom lip. My finger is now rubbing only on her clit. OMG her clit hard and wet! She is so wet that my finger slides right ino her pussy. She lets out a whimper. I slide another finger in her juicy pussy. Another whimper but this time her knees buckle. I turn her around and gently nibble on her nipples. She's begging me for more. Keisha sits on the edge of the bed legs wide open and I get down and devour her sweet peach pussy. One hand pinching, pulling her titty nipples. The other hand behind her back pulling her into my face even more. I suck on her clit which drives her crazy, "Oh MY FUCKIN GOD GIGI IM CUMIN! PLEASE DON'T STOP!" I let my tongue twirl in and out of her pussy while pulling her in closer and she starts to shake "OH SHIT YES YES YES YESSSSSSSSS OOOOOOHHHHHHHHH OOOOHHHHHHH" Keisha then snatches away and falls back on the bed. Breathing heavy trying to catch her breath, shaking her head mumbling, "Wow that was amazing!" While she still in shock I grab the strapon, turn the rose to level 3 and put it on her clit. Then I slide the strapon right into her drippin wet tight pussy. She grabs my titties while her eyes roll in the back of her head. I'm givin her long strokes. Rose is now at max level. "GIGI, GIGI, I I I"...I put my finger over her lips and say "shhh just enjoy baby, relax and let go." She looked me in my eyes and laid back arching her back, letting out multiple moans of ecstasy. I know I hit the right spot cause she now has her nails in my back. Pushing her legs back and go in deeper into her wet pussy. "Oh GIGI baby you the beeeessssssttttt!" She cums soo hard, that her pussy tightens up gripping the dildo, pushes it out and starts creamin everywhere.

While she still cumin I slide the double end dildo in my soaking wet pussy then hers. Now we scissoring with the dildo rubbing each other titties til we both scream out in passion and squirt on each other at the same time.

Twan

"So Twan, what do you have planned for your bday?"

"Nothing working."

"You ain't got nothing special planned?"

"Nope just working."

"Well what about Saturday?"

"That afternoon i'm busy, but free that evening."

"Ok cool, well you not free anymore."

"What's that suppose to mean?"

"I just booked a jacuzzi room at

NIJO SUITES, you can bring a friend if you want."

"Gigi don't fuckin play with me!"

"Twan i'm serious"

"Aight bet! Send me the info i'll be there, and i'll bring the drink."

"See you saturday."

I get off the phone with Twan excited as fuck. I got 2 days to get my shit together.

To Do List: Hit the dispensary for some edibles, grab some water, and something sexy to wear. Yup this gonna be a birthday he will never forget!

𝕏 𝕏

Damn it's saturday already. Time to get this show on the road.

"Hey Twan your key is at the front desk room number 124 see you soon." So I get the jacuzzi ready, get in just relaxing when he walks in...

"Damn baby you started without me?"

"Naw just getting relaxed for you."

"Well ol girl should be here shortly."

Knock Knock "damn you wasn't lying" he opens the door.

"Gigi this Ashley"

"Hey girl, aw shit you got the jacuzzi ready let me strip so I can get in"

"Come ON!" So me and Ashley making small talk and I pop a edible along with a terpine shot.

"Oh shit is that a edible let me get

one"

"Sure girl" Now my edible from earlier done kicked in (yes I have to pregame fuckin with Twan) and my pussy is hot and wet. I start rubbing Ashley thighs and she sucks my nipples. Twan comes out the bathroom and ain't say a word, he just grabbed the bottle of Hennessy and poured 3 shots. We toast to him and throw it back, now they chasing it with cranberry juice but you know how ya girl get down so I tell Twan naw i'm good baby. Ashley puts her glass down and starts nimbling on my ear. That turned Twan on cause next thing I know he standing in front of us butt ball naked, dick at straight attention. That muthafucka was looking so delicious with that curve, I swear it was winking at me. We do 2 more shots, me and Ashley get out the jacuzzi. I kiss Twan and tell him have a seat and enjoy the show. He poured another shot but this time she punked out saying she was done, so me and him toast to a good as night to come. Before I could put my glass down good she pulls me down on the bed and begins to eat my pussy. It felt ok nothing spectacular, my rose does a better job, but he watching so I faked like the shit felt good. She comes up for air. She turns over, spreading her legs and I begin licking them pussy lips and sucking her clit. I slide not 1 but 2 fingers in her pussy making the come here motion, she starts cummin and then pushes my head away.

"Hey we suppose to be pleasuring

Twan" so he comes and lays in the middle of the bed. Ashley decides she gonna run the show so I step back and watch her suck his dick. She stroking his shaft and sucking the tip "Oh shit Twan thats too much dick to be going in anybody mouth." Gets up smiling and sits in the chair. 'Oh it's my turn now?' I kiss his balls then let my tongue go up his dick to the head. This bitch think she really did something, yea ok. I open my mouth and go down on his dick letting slob drip on his balls. My head bobbing up and down slow, one hand rubbing his chest the other caressing his balls. I'm suckin, hummin, slobbin on his dick all at once, and he's moanin. I relax my throat and his dick slides all the way down my esophagus, to the point that I now have his balls in my mouth. Sucking his dick making plunger sounds. Yea this that shit! I knew I hit his spot cause this nigga sat up like he was rising from the dead. I'm looking him in his eyes and he's staring back at me in amazement like, WTF! My throat releases the grip on his dick and all the slob just falls all over my titties. I bend over perfect arch and he slowly inserts his 12 inch curve in my dripping wet pussy. 2 strokes and i'm squirting, he still stroking...I'm screaming loud.....

"BABY I'M CUMMIN"

"Naw baby it's too early for all that!" smacks my ass and pulls my hair, I started squirting even more. The bed has officially been soaked! My pussy ain't been fuck'd like this in months. The bed is so wet he making me crawl to a dry spot while still fuckin my ocean wet pussy, never pulling out. He gives my ass another smack so hard it echoed. Flips me over snatches me to the edge of the bed, throws my legs over his shoulders and rams his dick inside of me. I swear he hit my spot so hard that I levitated off the bed.

"Baby please dont stop fuckin me!"

By now we both done forgot all about Ashley and she realizes this. She goes in the bathroom claiming to be sick. But me and Twan so lost in each other we keep fuckin. He then puts his hand around my neck, that shit turned me on so much that I pulled my legs behind my head. His eyes lock on me, he didn't have to say a word you could read his face "Really it's like that, bet!" Twan went waaaaay deep til he hit 'THE' spot. I started cummin, creamin, and squirting so much it was splashing in his face. All of a sudden we hear Ashley screamin. He stops fuckin me to check on her. She all in her feelings and shit, trying to start a argument with him. Now Twan is not a arguing man so he let her say what was on her mind. I intervened trying to calm the situation but this bitch was drunk and high. She was so fuck'd up she couldn't see straight. So I went and put my clothes on. They follow behind me now everybody dressed. Mind you it's only 7pm. We had just started drinking around 5:30. She leaves and he follows her outside. Twan comes back 10 mins later "Hey baby drive her car to her house and i'll bring you back here". That shit blew me so much, I wasn't done fuckin and this bitch interrupted my dick. "Yea baby ok". So this bitch stayed in Firstville and we were in Avon Lake. A hour drive to say the least, and being heavily intoxicated shiddd, but anything to get her ass gone. ******2hours later me and Twan back at the room. I filled the jacuzzi again and got in to calm my nerves. I was pissed cause I knew he was leaving, but to my surprise he strips and gets in with me. He was so frustrated that his veins were popping out his forehead and neck. Twan was venting, venting, but it was turning me on. I massaged his temples as he talked. That wasn't working. What can I do to calm this man? Now you know black women don't get their hair wet for no reason whats so ever. Well I hated to see him so upset. So while he was talking I took in a deep breath and let his dick slide in my mouth. Yes i'm giving him head under water. I came up for a breath and went down and swallowed his dick again. When I came up for air this time he grabbed me, pulled me close, and gave me the longest most sensual kiss you could ever imagine. His tongue was soft like cotton candy, lips so juicy I didn't want him to stop. He got up and reached for my hand so he could help me out. He wrapped them muscle arms around me and laid me down gently on the bed. Kissing me from my ears, neck, lips, sucked both breast, taking his tongue down my navel, spreading my legs, kissing my thighs, and back over to my pussy. He talked to her, massaged her, licked her slow, tongue kissed my clit til I came. Lifted my legs, put my toes in his mouth sucking each one slow as he slid his dick in my now tight wet pussy. Yes I got that good snapback! We were no longer fucking. He looked in my eyes and kissed me long and hard with each stroke. It was so intense we came together telling each other "I love you baby".........

Staycation

I'm so damn bored. I need something to do. Why would I take a vacation and not make any plans? I could call over Tae, hmm do I really want some dick? I know i'm not the only woman who has felt like this. These are the thoughts running thru my mind as I sit on the balcony over looking the beach. I hear all these people laughing my ass should be down there. Oh that is a sexy nig... wait that's a female? A stud? She sexy as hell but I dont care for studs.. That's it I haven't been with a woman in a while. Yea I need a girlfriend. I've been looking for months but no luck, guess i'll check this dating site i'm on. So I log in and sure enough I have over 20 messages from women. None of these women fit my criteria and if they do they are too far away.. Wait a minute she's cute and not that far. Ok lets see what's to her.

Amber: Hello Gina, you are very attractive and I would like to get to know you. If you are interested hmu 969-6969

Well damn that's what i'm talkin bout. So you know I texted her.

"Hi Amber this is Gina, but my friends call me Gigi. So tell me what you are looking for and what made you want to give me your number"

"Hi Gigi, you are FINE and you have some HUGE titties. To be completely honest your picture made me wet as fuck and I wanna eat your pussy. Did that answer your question?"

"Well damn Amber, that left me speechless but my titties are BIG! I play with them myself alot, even suck them too sometimes LOL. I'm free today if you want to meet up for drinks and grab something to eat..."

"That's cool but I wanted to eat your pussy, so how bout I eat your pussy first that way I can get full off you so that's less food I order.. lol naw but for real"

"Shit ok then. I live in a apartment with a balcony that overlooks the beach. It's a beautiful site. So you can come here or I can come to you"

"Send me the address and I'll be on my way"

Gigi just started sharing location with you*

"Ok I got it be there in about a hour."

"Ok see you soon"

Shit I can't believe this I'm finally bout be pleased by a woman after all this time. I can take a quick shower, eat a edible so it will have kicked in, yesss can't wait.

***Hour later my phone rings and it's Amber telling me she is here. I tell her take the elevator to the 12th fl apartment 693. Hang up the phone and 2minutes later I hear the elevator doors open so I unlock my door. In walks this 5'7, butterscotch complected, shoulder length black hair, 46 DD, 32 waist, 44 hip woman. This chic was fine and my pussy instantly got wet. She hugs me and I lead her straight to my bedroom.

"So Gigi what do you think?"

"Amber your are so fine, you have to let me taste you first, its been months since I was with a woman."

"Well Gigi I guess you can feast on me first. And i've never squirted before."

"That sounds like a challenge. I love challenges. I accept!

Amber takes all of her clothes off and just stands in front of me. Her perky gumdrop caramel nipples poking straight out. I fondled both her titties putting the left tittie in my mouth, sucking on her nipple like it's a bottle. She must've like the way I was doing it cause I now feel her fingers sliding in and out of my pussy I was about to cum but I pulled away.

"Lay down in the middle of the bed."
Amber climbed in the bed and laid down. She spread her legs open and there was the prettiest pussy I've ever seen. It was glistenin with her juices, clit sticking out. I put my tongue in her pussy lickin all her wetness. Moving my tongue in and out of her slowly, then up to her hard clit licking round and round, teasing it with my tongue, now sucking it. I feel my chin getting wet from her cummin. I keep suckin on her clit while I move my chin on her pussy. She feels the sensation and starts to cum harder. Letting the clit go I bury my entire face in her pussy shakin

my head from side to side real fast with my tongue hittin those spots. Her legs begin to tremble, reaching up playing with her nipples, she grabs the back of my head and lets out a loud moan "Gigi this feels so good i'm cummin" letting my tongue go deeper in her pussy making her squirt all over my face. Shaking my head even faster it's splashing everywhere, even got in my hair. With her legs steady shaking I reach over and grab my dildo. Now this not a plain dildo this that rotating shaft with stroke motion. I put the dildo in with it on stroke motion. Now she's really moaning. I turn around and 69 her. Riding her face while the dildo stroking her. That muthafucka had to be on her g-spot cause the way she was eating my pussy I could have passed out. She got her nose all in my pussy while suckin my clit. Oh she can't make me squirt fuck that! Turning the dildo on max speed and licking on that clit made her cum so damn hard. Between creamin and squirtin not only did it shoot up in my face but the dildo flew clean across the room. That shit turned me on so much that I sat up on her tongue riding it grabbin her titties and squirting all over her face, I mean it was everywhere, up her nose, in her eyes, hair, mouth, sliding down her neck. Oh yes this chic can eat some pussy! She can have it anytime she wants. I get off her face and she kisses me.

"Gigi, yea you are a fuckin beast with that tongue I ain't never had my pussy ate like that before. Yea ima definitely keep in contact with you. I don't feel like going out to eat now i'm tired how bout we go next weekend?"

"Ok sounds like a plan to me."

I give her a towel to wash up, throw on some clothes and walk her to her car, she kisses me and tells me she'll text me when she get home. I go back in my apartment and run me a nice hot bath. Relaxing in the tub thinking about how this woman just devoured my pussy like it was her last meal ever. Nobody has ever made me cum that fuckin hard just from licking my clit. She is at the top of my list. Hell she keep it up I might have to stop fuckin with Twan. Yea she just that good that it will make you switch teams completely..

****

My phone goes off and it's 7am. That girl fucked me so good it put me to sleep, I don't even know if she made it home. I look at my phone 2 unread messages and 1 missed call. Well at least I know she made it home. 1 unread message

"Good morning wyd"

"I'm just waking up what's up with you stranger?"

"Aww don't be like that, just been busy. Do you even know who this is?"

"Yea I do. Greg a ghost from the past."

"I wanna see you like right now"

"Give me a minute to wash my ass and get dressed"

"All I want is to see you, and i'll even come to you so you can stay comfortable."

"Aight come on, can I at least brush my teeth?" Damn no reply. Ok, well I know it'll take him atleast 20minutes I got time to hop in the shower. Soon as I stuck my leg in the water there's a knock at my door. I look out the peephole and there is Greg. 6'7 high yellow with hazel and grey eyes. Soon as he hear the lock click he pushed the door open and wrapped his arms around me picking me up off the floor. He put me down and we just sat and talked catching up. It's been about 3 years since i've seen him. Still looking good and he know it too cause I was staring at him as he talked licking my lips. He tried to ignore me but couldn't. After about 45mins of not paying attention to what he was saying Greg stood up to leave. You know this man had got me hot and all I had on was a robe. I walked over to him trying to grab his dick but he stopped me.

"What you doing?"

"I just want to see it"

"Nope I just wanted to see you and give you a hug"

"Bullshit! I need some dick! I got fucked good by this chic last night but I still need some dick to complete me."

"Gigi yo ass crazy i'm bout to go!"

I walked up on him, grab his hand and stuck his fingers in my pussy.

"OH SHHIT it's so damn wet. WTF are you doing so damn wet?"

As he saying this he's walking me to my bedroom backwards. Pushes me down on the bed, push my legs back and slides his dick in my pussy. It felt so damn good. He start giving me long hard strokes. He licks his fingers and rubs my clit while still stroking. I'm shaking and he looks down and sees his dick getting whiter and whiter with each stroke. Before my legs can go limp he gets up and walks off. I follow behind him barely able to stand.

"Whats wrong with you?"

"You just gonna do me like that and leave. I was still cummin and you just stop. Thats some foul shit!"

I turned my back on him and he grabs me from behind and bends me over. He rams his hard dick in my pussy (Now Greg dick is about 8inchs, much smaller than what i'm used to with Tae and Twan) smackin my ass trying to make me squirt. Little does he know he will never make me squirt cause his dick don't touch my spot. But he gives it that good ol try. Greg is about to cum so he pulls out, squeezes his dick and just stood there. I'm like "what is you doing?" "I'm stoppin myself from nuttin."

 "I ain't never heard of that but yea ok." He puts his dick up and saids

"Ok now I really gotta go" kisses me and walks out the door. I'm standing there with a wet pussy ready to explode and this nigga leaves. I wanted to call Tae to finish the job but I'll wait. Oh fuck i'm not suppose to be doing shit cause I have a dick appointment with Twan in the morning. Ok let me explain, I make it a rule to never fuck anybody else the day before I see Twan. Well Greg ain't all that big so I should be ok. Just soak in some epsom salt and i'll be fine. I'm putting my phone on do not disturb so I don't get into anymore trouble. Poured me a glass of wine and watched tv til tv watched me.

****

I wake up to the sound of thunder, oh wait it's not raining that's Twans text tone

"Baby i'm down stairs"

"Ok, I'll leave the door unlocked"

Twan walks in and immediately starts stripping leaving a trail of clothes all the way to the bedroom.

"Hey baby, I see you got on my favorite color red. You know I been missing you."

"I miss you too Twan. You can't be keepin my friend away from me like that"

"Well you gonna tell him hi?" my red lace teddy hits the floor
I lay a long kiss on those juicy lips of his and he sits on the bed. Dropping to my knees, kissing the tip of his dick, licking the sides up and down making sure to get it completely wet. (Remember ladies plenty of lubrication is the key to a successful dick suck.) Sucking the

tip of his dick while swirling my tongue thinking about how I was eating Amber pussy last night. With her pussy on my mind my tongue went crazy on Twan dick, got his toes curling reaching for shit that ain't even there. Going down slowly on his dick while staring up at him making his dick curve even more. I mean that muthafucka was gangbangin to the left so damn hard in my throat, straight chokin me, but i'm not stoppin cause I know baby be missing this. I got control of that curve and once he touched my tonsil and felt me gag he fell back on the bed looking at all the slob that fell on my tits.

"Come sit that wet ass pussy on this dick!"

Shit after damn near killing me

hell yea i'm riding yo ass! Climbing on top of him trying to ease down but instead he grabs my waist and snatches me down making sure that curve go all the way up in my stomach. That felt so good I got super wet. Rolling my hips real slow, caressing his balls and staring him in his eyes. Both my 42G titties in his hands, flicking his fingers over my nipples, sitting up to suck my titties. I push him back down "Naw naw, i'm running this!" Putting his hands back around my waist gliding me up and down on his dick mid stroke with that curve hittin my spot, my pussy grippin his dick, i'm moving up and down even faster, calling his name creaming everywhere, I lean over and kiss him, he kisses me back sticking his tongue in my mouth still holding my waist making me cum so hard that it brings me to a screaming orgasm. I started riding him so fast that we both came at the sametime, swear I heard the headboard crack. Laying on his chest trying not to go to sleep.

"Hey baby i'm kinda sticky"

I get up grab a towel and wipe him off. Grab 2 shot glasses and pour some Henny.

"Naw baby not tonight I gotta go in to work soon, take my shot for me. I have some beer anyway. You got me right?"

"Yea baby you know I do"

I take the double shot and grab the bottle of water cause that shit was strong. I'm rubbing that curve and he say "Hey baby you broke that muthafucka, him dead". I look up at him and while massaging his dick I tell him about me and Amber. His dick steady growing in my hand, "look like him ain't dead" Twan stands up bends me over, tongue kisses my pussy and slides his dick right in. All I feel is his balls slappin my clit. One hand pushing my ass up, the other hand on my shoulder pulling me in closer. This nigga went deep sea diving in my pussy. That curve hitting my spot each time. Pushing my face into the mattress, putting one leg on the bed pound driving tha fuck outta my pussy. The next stroke he went all the way in grabbing and holding me so close that I could feel every inch of his dick, every drop of nut that he just shot in me. Stepping back smackin my ass "Damn baby i'm tired told

you know I have to work tonight, yo ass be trynna kill a nigga".
My phone won't stop going off so I check it and have 10 missed calls and 5 unread messages all from Tae. Oh shit Twan was supposed to had been gone 2hrs ago.

"......Hey I been trying to call you to see if you ate yet but you ain't answering the phone"

"You must be sleep"

"Hello! have you eaten what do you want?"

"I'm picking up a pizza"

"Be there in 30mins................"

    "SHIT SHIT SHIT!" is what came out my mouth.

"Gi baby what's wrong? Look i'm bout to bounce I gotta go get ready for work."

I ain't realize Twan had picked up his clothes and was completely dressed. "Ok baby", I walked him to the door and he walks out sprinting to the elevator.. "Aye no goodbye kiss?" He turns and blows me a kiss disappearing around the corner. Fuck I gotta hurry up and wash my ass and get his scent out. Scent removal is easy. Just use Mold and Mildew shower spray in the air and on the walls that will hide any smell. (You welcome for the info just put ya on game lol). Ok so smell gone, spray fabric refresher on the bed, hop in the shower put the sprayer directly on my pussy as hot as I can take it. Jump out the shower, dry off, spray on some perfume and put back on the same red teddy and lay in the bed.

About 20minutes past and I start dosing off. All of a sudden lips are kissing my forehead.

"Hey baby I figured you were sleep and look at you, I was right knocked out, even got a little drool hanging lol. I don't know if you got my text I grabbed a pizza."
(Yes Tae has a key, and I know ya think i'm crazy having sexcapades and he got a key. But when ya man got a job that once clocked in he can't leave and you have his schedule, him having a key don't matter. It's for his security that way you can have your freedom.. Knowledge ladies they do it to us..)
Now i'm still horny and wet from Twan. Tae strips down and hops in the shower. I take another shot of Hennessy. Tae gets out the shower, pushes me up against the wall

kneels down, puts my leg over his shoulder kissing my inner thigh til he gets to my pussy lips and sucks on them, grabbin my ass pulling me into his face. My knees buckle cause i'm already weak from Twan. Tae wraps my legs around his neck, picks me up still eating my pussy and puts me down on the bed. With my legs still in the air he lifts me up and puts his dick inside of me. I was super tight, that's what snapback pussy is. Tae hitting all my spots even the ones Twan missed. Tae pushed my legs all the way in the bed making me cum, putting his hand around my throat making me squirt uncontrollably.

"I know that nigga was over here fuckin you"

I look up at Tae and he has rage

and ecstasy in his eyes.

"Gina don't lie I saw him come out the door and you asked bout a fuckin kiss. Yea I saw all that shit!"

The whole time he still fuckin me and it felt so good. Pissed off dick is great lbvs. Well I was caught no need in lying now..

"Yea Tae I fuckd him."

"So you call yourself having a side nigga? Bet he don't fuck you like this!"
Tae let my neck go, put his arm underneath my back scooped me up and had me in mid air blowin my back out.

"I know he ain't hit it like this did he?"

Barely able to utter a word "No"

"No what?"

"No daddy"

"Whats my name?"

"Daddy"

"Say it again louder"

"DADDY"

"Now say his name you know you want too, gone head."

Me not thinking and the way Tae had my ass shaking and cummin I called out Twan name. That made Tae dick even harder. He pulls his dick out, flips me over and start tagging me from the back. Grabbin a handful of hair pummeling my pussy.

"IMMA FUCK YOU LIKE HE SHOULD HAVE!"

Tae pounding my pussy so hard I fall on the bed, "oh you ain't done" spreadin my cheeks licking my ass, fingering me, rubbin the cum on my asshole so he can slide in.

"Yea I know he ain't get this ass. Who this ass belong to? Oh no answer."

Tae sees my dildo grabs it and puts it in my pussy on max speed. Dick in my ass and pussy at the sametime.

"Now who you belong to?"

"D.A.D.D.Y!"

"Say my FUCKIN NAME!"

"Dontae!"

"Spell that shit!"

"DDDD (smacks my ass again)

"Spell that shit right!"

"DDONTTtttTTTAAEEEEEEEEEEE EEEEEEEE" (with every ounce of energy he had, when I said that last letter of his name he went so far in my ass I lost my hearing)

Tae nutted so damn hard that when he pulled out he was still nuttin all over my ass. I rolled over looked at him and couldn't do or say nothing. I watched Tae walk into the bathroom and start the shower.. he turns and looks at me and saids.....

"Now that's real side nigga dick! If you gonna fuck off atleast make sure the nigga can fuck up your understanding!"

To be continued........

Made in the USA
Columbia, SC
30 August 2024

41323223R00074